Guide to the
Good Life

BY SIMCHA WHITEHILL

Scholastic

All rights reserved. Published by Scholastic Inc., *Publishers since 1920*. SCHOLASTIC and associated logos are trademarks and/or registered trademarks of Scholastic Inc.

The publisher does not have any control over and does not assume any responsibility for author or third-party websites or their content.

This book is a work of fiction. Names, characters, places, and incidents are either the product of the author's imagination or are used fictitiously, and any resemblance to actual persons, living or dead, business establishments, events, or locales is entirely coincidental.

ISBN 978-1-339-01649-8

10 9 8 7 6 5 4 3 2 1   24 25 26 27 28

Printed in the U.S.A.   40

This edition first printing 2024

Designed by Cheung Tai

CONTENTS

YOUR JOURNEY

Life is a journey, as every Trainer and Pokémon knows. You have to Rock Climb every mountain, Scratch every itch, Tackle every challenge, and learn to roll with the Focus Punches. If Pokémon can do it, so can you!

This book will show you how to master the fine art of living, and living well—just like a Pokémon!

GOOD LOOKS

Just like you put the "you" in unique, every Pokémon species has its own individual look. Pokémon know how to take pride in their appearance and use it as an advantage on and off the battlefield. It's called style. They know that to live your best life, you've gotta rock what ya got!

Some Pokémon are Scaly.

MAGIKARP

JANGMO-O

VIVILLON

Some are Slimy.

GOOM

MUK

Some are furry.

FURFROU

EEVEE

GROWLITHE

Some have feathers.

TORCHIC

HO-OH

PIDGEOT

Some are fluffy.

WHIMSICOTT

JUMPLUFF

MAREEP

Some are fiery.

CHARMANDER

CYNDAQUIL

PONYTA

Some have wings.

DRAGONITE

BUTTERFREE

BEAUTIFLY

Some have teeth.

BIDOOF

GLALIE

Some have claws.

TEDDIURSA

WEAVILE

Some have horns.

PINSIR

DUBWOOL

Some have blades for arms.

SCYTHER

KRICKETUNE

Some have shells.

DWEBBLE

SQUIRTLE

Lots of Pokémon have tails . . .

FENNEKIN

Some have springy tails.

GLAMEOW

Some have handy tails.

AIPOM

Some have a bunch of tails.

VULPIX

Some have a *whole* bunch of tails— nine, to be exact!

NINETALES

Some Pokémon are bald . . .

DUGTRIO

Some Pokémon are blond . . .

ALOLAN DUGTRIO

Some Pokémon have no head!

STARMIE

Some Pokémon have 2 heads . . .

WEEZING

BINACLE

DODUO

Some Pokémon have 3 heads . . .

HYDREIGON

COMBEE

DODRIO

Some Pokémon have 2 x 3 heads.

(That's 6 heads!)

EXEGGCUTE

Some Pokémon Look Like a Tree . . .

Not a tree.

SUDOWOODO

BONSLY

Not a tree.

Not a tree.

TREVENANT

Also not a tree.

EXEGGUTOR

Not a tree.

ALOLAN EXEGGUTOR

Not a tree . . . Wait, those *are* actual trees on Torterra's back!

TORTERRA

Some Pokémon Look Like Poké Balls . . .

But don't try to throw them. You can, however, try to catch them . . . with a Poké Ball.

Foongus looks like one Poké Ball.

FOONGUS

Amoonguss looks like three.

And it will stand next to Poké Balls to blend in. Sneaky!

AMOONGUSS

Electrode looks like a big Poké Ball.

But at 146.8 pounds, it'd be a lot harder to throw!

ELECTRODE

Galarian Stunfisk's lips look like a Poké Ball.

It uses them to lure in prey—or humans. Consider yourself warned!

GALARIAN STUNFISK

Electric-type Voltorb try to blend in as Poké Balls.

But if their unusual size doesn't shock you, their attacks will.

Some Pokémon Look Like Food . . .

But don't try to eat them!

CHERUBI

SLURPUFF

APPLIN

BOUNSWEET

VANILLITE

Pokémon know that making and eating good food is one of the true joys of life! If you have to do it at least three times a day, you might as well enjoy it. Here's how to live well by eating well, like a Pokémon!

OODLES OF NOODLES

When life hands you claws . . .

Make ramen!
Really, really good ramen.

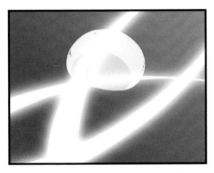
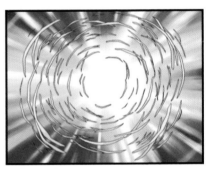

FOOD FIGHT

Ketchup tastes good on everything.

Ketchup also tastes good with nothing.

Ash's Pikachu loves ketchup. Its favorite sauce is useful at mealtime—and even at battle time!

Scyther slashed,

Pikachu blocked,

and . . .

Splat! Ketchup in the face.

A SWEET MOVE

You never know where your skills might end up being useful.

A Raichu named Sugar uses Focus Punch to crack open the special ingredient in its baked goods: Aspear Berries. Yum!

HOW TO CATCH A POKÉMON WITH A SANDWICH

First, you'll need a sandwich, cut in half.

Then, give both halves of the sandwich to the Pokémon you want to catch. Now its hands will be too full to battle.

Quick, toss your Poké Ball!

Success!

WASTE NOT, WANT NOT

The way to a Pokémon's heart is through its stomach.

There's just nothing as yummy as a meal cooked especially for you!

Even when you don't love what you've prepared, don't throw it out. Someone else might like it!

Most of May's friends were not fans of her "Purple Surprise" . . .

But Munchlax loved it!

One person's trash is Garbodor's treasure! Garbodor, the Trash Heap Pokémon, eats trash—not junk food, actual junk. It turns waste into vicious Poison-type attacks.

And vicious burps!

TAKES THE CAKE

Food can pave the way for getting what you want!

Ash found the best chocolate cake in Brackish Town.

It's so good that when he shared a bite with Diantha—the Champion of the Kalos region— she agreed to battle him!

THE ICING ON THE CAKE

Flavor is important, but don't underestimate
the power of a cute-looking cake.

Alcremie's sweet cream can help you make
a cake look *and* taste good!

But be careful about eating too much of the finished product . . .

If you're too full to battle, you might get creamed!

"Feast-a-max" Pikachu learned this the hard way.

MOR IS MOR

You might not be your best self when you're hungry. Take it from Morpeko.

It's happy when it's in Full Belly Mode.

But when Morpeko needs to eat, it goes into Hangry Mode . . .

And if you don't share your food with it,
it might fry you to a crisp!

Put the Fast in Breakfast

Pokémon know that if the prize for a contest is food, they'd better start practicing!

The winner of the Pokémon Pancake Race in Alola gets a year's supply of breakfast pancakes.

To compete, Trainers and their Pokémon run through Melemele Island carrying a plate of pancakes.

They need speed.

They need balance.

It's tough to keep all those pancakes stacked up!

Though sometimes, they just need luck—like Komala, who won the race in its sleep!

WE ALL SCREAM FOR ICE CREAM

If you're looking forward to getting a treat,
like ice cream . . .

Be sure to check that the shop is
open before you go.

BETTER TOGETHER

Pokémon know that whatever
you're eating . . .

The best food is a meal you share
with friends!

GOOD FUN

In your free time, don't just sit there twiddling your thumbs—go have fun! Take a hint from these hobbies Pokémon love . . .

DANCING

Turn your battlefield into a dance floor, and groove your way to victory!

Bust a move while you dodge moves, like
Tierno and Ludicolo . . .

If the rhythm doesn't strike you,
their attacks will!

Even if you lose the battle,
your swagger will win over the crowd!

If you can dance and sing at the same time, you're made for the stage! Try musical theater.

Even if there is almost no one in the audience, the show must go on!

MOVIES

If you prefer the screen to the stage, you can act in a movie! Zorua is a master at transforming itself for a role.

(Can you believe that blond princess was really Zorua?! What an actor!)

Or you can make videos of yourself and become a social media star.

Or you might direct your own movie!

If you don't want to make movies,
you can watch movies. That's also a hobby!

LEARNING SOMETHING NEW

You can learn anything if you put your mind to it and put in the work!

After all, Meowth is a Pokémon that taught itself to walk like a human . . .

Dress like a human . . .

And talk like a human.

And now Meowth is funnier than any human!

PAINTING

Try painting, like Smeargle.

Smeargle paint whenever and wherever they can. Including on buildings . . .

Or on people!

Some people don't mind being part of the art.

Different strokes for different folks!

SWIMMING

Jump right in and swim! You might prefer to train hard in the water . . .

Or just go with the flow.

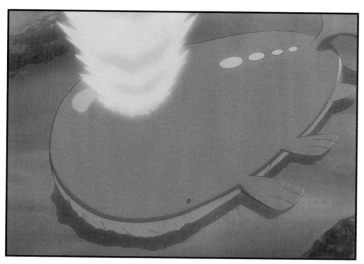

TREASURE HUNTING

You could try following your nose to find hidden treasure, like Stoutland!

You might find a rare berry . . .

Or dig up a cool Cranidos fossil . . .

Or just score some junk.

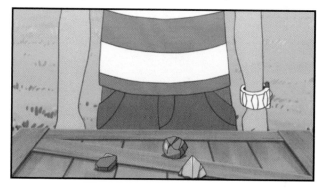

But be sure to share your finds with friends.
One person's junk is another person's treasure!

PLAYING AN INSTRUMENT

Learn to make some music on an instrument! You can practice and have fun playing alone . . .

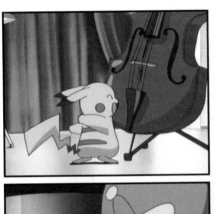

Or jam in a band together with friends!

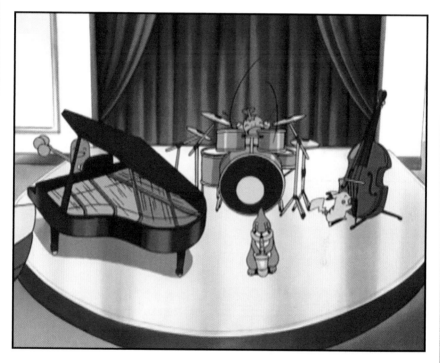

MAKING MAGIC

You can become a magician! All you need is a top hat, a wand . . .

And to learn some magic tricks!

Ta-da!

FASHION DESIGNING

Ever dreamed of making your own clothing?
Take a cue from Leavanny and learn to sew
snazzy outfits for you and your friends!

Some friends might not share your
fashion sense.

But others might be willing to wear your unique inspirations!

MIMING

If you like using your imagination, then you might like miming.

And if you truly believe what you're doing, like Mr. Mime . . .

That wall might just become real!

SINGING

You can learn to sing!

Perform a beautiful solo and audiences
will adore you.

Or, if you're Jigglypuff, you might just put them to sleep.

And when your audience is dozing, you might be tempted to draw on their faces . . .

But hopefully they won't mind their new look!

Singing with friends is nice, too!

But if your friend draws on *your* face while *you're* asleep from their singing . . .

Make sure your attitude about it is as good as Jigglypuff's!

Jigglypuff knows: Don't dish it if you can't take it.

GOOD SLEEP

Pokémon know that the best way to power up is to get some serious shut-eye. You can't play well without sleeping well! So start counting Mareep . . .

SLEEPING BEAUTIES

where can you Sleep?
Wherever is comfy!

Some Pokémon like to camp out under the stars.

Some Pokémon like to rest in a cozy bed.

Rowlet likes to nap in Ash's backpack.

Delcatty can sleep anywhere!

When can you sleep?
However long feels right!

Abra sleeps eighteen hours a day. The deeper Abra sleeps, the farther it can teleport.

Komala always seems to be asleep.

It doesn't just sleep *like* a log—it sleeps *on* a log.

And if it doesn't have a log, it'll sleep on something else—like Professor Samson Oak's head.

Komala can sleep through anything! It can eat while it sleeps . . .

It can ring the school bell while it sleeps . . .

It can even fight back while it sleeps.

Komala knows: don't let anything get between you and your precious rest!

How do you get to sleep?
However you need to!

Snorlax needs to eat 880 pounds
of food to go to sleep!

That's roughly the weight of three Ursaring.
Or one whole Wailord!

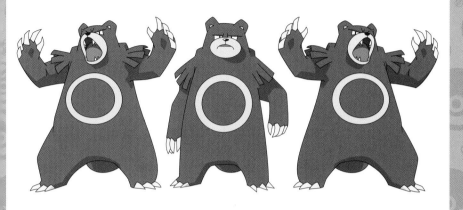

GOOD BATTLES

Just like in Pokémon battles, competition with others can be fun, but there are some basic rules to follow to make sure everyone has a good time.

First, make sure you train with whoever's on your side until you become a truly terrific team.

Don't forget to always be polite.
Good manners go a long way!

When it's time to start, be ready to go.
Then, give it your all!

No matter how big the challenge,
don't get discouraged.

Be creative as you compete! You might
combine skills you know, or try something
totally new.

But no matter if you win or lose,
it's how you play the game.

And when you're finished, look ahead
to the next challenge!

GOOD EGGS

What's more egg-citing than new life?!
Pokémon Eggs are precious. There's a lot to
learn from them!

Every Egg is unique.

And they're all fragile, so be gentle with them.
(A hug-proof case can help!)

Whether you find one . . .

Win one . . .

Or get one as a gift . . .

You never know what might result from it!

Be patient. Eggs will hatch when they're ready.

In fact, some Pokémon (like Togepi)
might never be ready to fully leave their Egg!

You know an Egg is about to hatch
when it starts to glow . . .

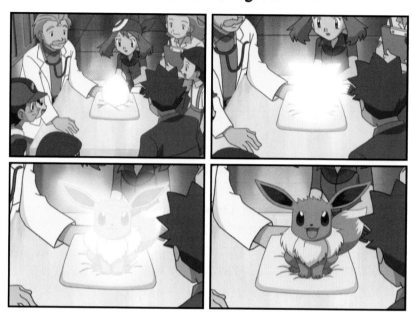

What comes out might
be your new best friend.

Now look who's
glowing!

GOOD QUESTION

If you dream it, you can achieve it! Take it
from Eevee, the Evolution Pokémon.
Eevee is a Normal type, but it can be
anything but normal! It is currently known
to become eight different evolved forms.
So the question is . . .

Which Eevee Evolution are you most like? Are you . . .

 Flashy and bold?
You're like Electric-type
JOLTEON!

 Fiery and fierce?
You're like Fire-type
FLAREON!

Cool as a cucumber?
You're like Ice-type
GLACEON!

 Adaptable and able
to totally **blend in?**
You're like Water-type
VAPOREON (who
disappears when it swims
in water)!

Happy to be
helpful?
You're like Grass-type
LEAFEON, who makes
clean air!

 A calm
peacemaker?
You're like Fairy-type
SYLVEON!

 Dark and
mysterious?
You're like Dark-type
UMBREON!

 Focused on the
future?
You're like Psychic-type
ESPEON!

GOOD FRIENDS

What's the ship that can carry
you through anything?
Friendship!

MAKING A FRIEND

Making a new friend is a rewarding challenge and a delicate process. You can't force it.

Pokémon know—just be yourself and be kind, and you're in business!

Not everyone is ready to be your friend at first . . .

This might shock you.

You can try to win them over,
but you must be patient.

Show them that you will be there
for them no matter what.

Show them that you care to earn their trust.

Once they see you're a good person, they'll be much more interested in friendship.

Then, maybe they'll help you, too!

If you're lucky, they'll end up being
your best friend forever.

And they might even help you
make more new friends!

THE ETERNAL FLAME OF FRIENDSHIP

Friends may come
(just in the nick of time!) . . .

And friends may go . . .

And sometimes friends come back again!

(When you reunite, make sure your greeting isn't *too* warm.)

With a true pal, no matter how much time has passed, you can always pick up right where you left off . . .

And make new memories.

Your bond will keep you close!

THE MORE THE MERRIER

Life is more fun with friends!

Have you ever wondered:
How many friends are too many?

One?

Two?

More?

Way more?

Answer:
You can never have too many friends!

The more the merrier.

TRUE FRIENDS

True friends are always rooting for you.

It doesn't matter if you win or lose. You'll always have their support!

The friends you surround yourself with matter.
With the right buddies by your side . . .

You will be winning at life!

GOOD ADVICE

How do you live your best life, according to Pokémon?

Dream big and don't give up! And, of course, be sure to make friends along the way.

There's no way we're giving up! That's not what we're about! We'll keep battling right up until the very end!